Wish upon a Starfish

★ Also by ★
Debbie Dadey

Mermaid Tales

Book 1: *Trouble at Trident Academy*

Book 2: *Battle of the Best Friends*

Book 3: *A Whale of a Tale*

Book 4: *Danger in the Deep Blue Sea*

Book 5: *The Lost Princess*

Book 6: *The Secret Sea Horse*

Book 7: *Dream of the Blue Turtle*

Book 8: *Treasure in Trident City*

Book 9: *A Royal Tea*

Book 10: *A Tale of Two Sisters*

Book 11: *The Polar Bear Express*

Coming Soon

Book 13: *The Crook and the Crown*

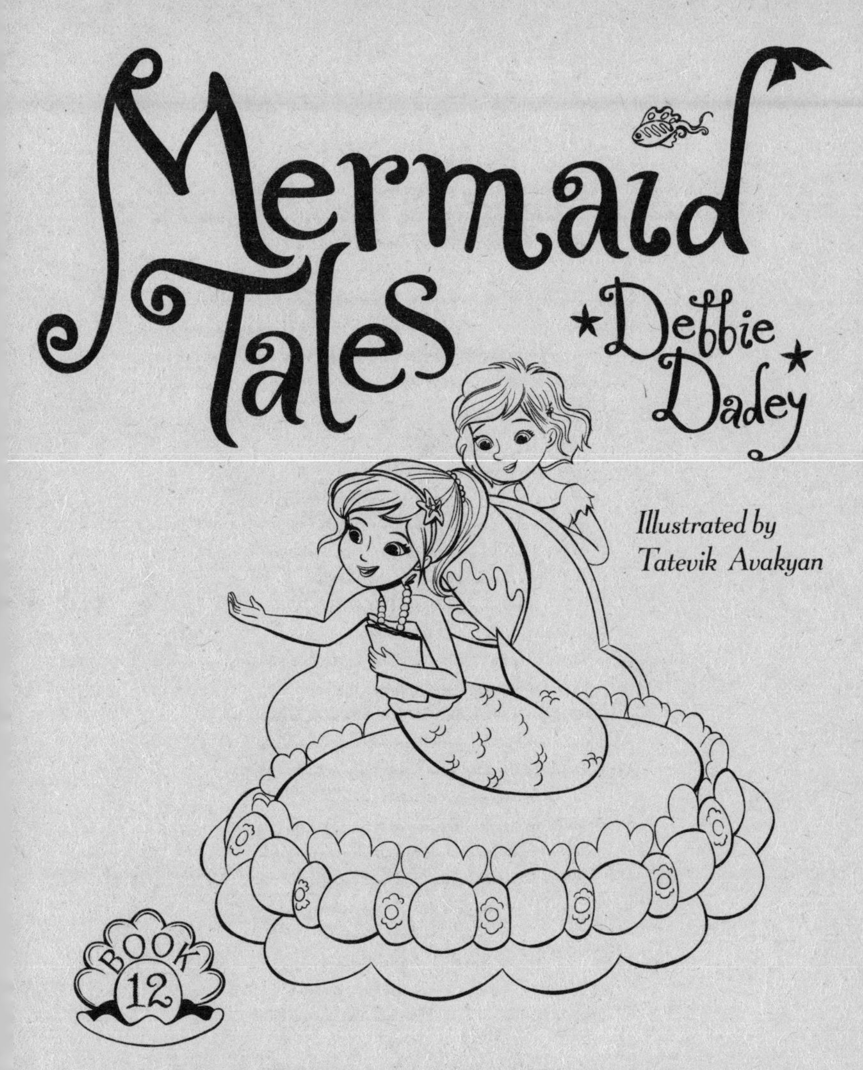

Wish upon a Starfish

ALADDIN
NEW YORK LONDON TORONTO SYDNEY NEW DELHI

ALADDIN
An imprint of Simon & Schuster Children's Publishing Division
1230 Avenue of the Americas, New York, NY 10020
This Aladdin paperback edition September 2015

Also available in an Aladdin hardcover edition.

For information about special discounts for bulk purchases,
please contact Simon & Schuster Special Sales at 1-866-506-1949
or business@simonandschuster.com.
The Simon & Schuster Speakers Bureau can bring authors to your live event.
For more information or to book an event contact the
Simon & Schuster Speakers Bureau at 1-866-248-3049
or visit our website at www.simonspeakers.com.
Series designed by Karin Paprocki
Cover designed by Karina Granda
The text of this book was set in Belucian Book.
Manufactured in the United States of America 1119 OFF
6 8 10 9 7 5
Library of Congress Control Number 2014958698
ISBN 978-1-4814-0264-4 (hc)
ISBN 978-1-4814-0263-7 (pbk)
ISBN 978-1-4814-0265-1 (eBook)

To Jasmine and Julie Eyal,

most observant readers ever

Acknowledgment

To Becky Dadey, most likely to steal the show.

N
E
S
W
The Mayor's House
Pearl's Home
Trident School for Languages
Trident City Hall
Big Rock Cafe
Trident Academy
Trident Plaza Hotel
The Coral Reef
56
Reef 56 Hotel
Merlin's
Angel Fish Antiques

Kelp Fields
Echo's House
People Museum • Shelly's Home
Manta Ray Station
Reef's Fish Store
MerPark
Little V
Whale Mountain
Big V
Trident City

Cast of Characters
Shelly
Echo
Kiki
Pearl
Rocky

Contents

Wish upon a Starfish

The Sound of Waves

"BRAVO!"

The crowd cheered and clapped as Pearl Swamp took a bow. Her diamond-studded costume billowed around her gold tail on the sparkling stage. Members of the audience whistled and tossed her beautiful bouquets of sea lavender.

Pearl waved as merfolk from all over the ocean cried out, "We love you, Pearl," and "You are the best actress in the whole merworld!"

She couldn't believe her good luck. A famous director had picked her out of all the merstudents at Trident Academy to star as Fishlein Maria in his play *The Sound of Waves*. As the curtain closed, a crowd of fans and reporters rushed to Pearl's side.

"Miss Swamp, may I have my picture sketched with you?" asked a small mergirl.

Pearl nodded and lifted her pointy nose in the water as the merartist Piddock Picasso sketched her on a piece of kelp for her fan.

Pearl

"May I have an interview?" asked *Trident City Tide* reporter Lulu Lampern.

"Of course," Pearl said, waving away the hundreds of merpeople still waiting to have their picture drawn with her. Others floated nearby, holding sea pens and seaweed, hoping Pearl would sign autographs.

"How does it feel to be famous?" Lulu asked.

Pearl smiled. "It is fabulous and everything I dreamed it would be."

Lulu scribbled some notes on seaweed before looking up. "What is your favorite part of being a star?"

"There is nothing more fin-tastic than knowing an audience is cheering for me,"

Pearl said. "It is an amazing feeling!" She paused before adding, "Of course, the jewels and flowers are nice too."

"You were simply mervelous in the play tonight," Lulu said. "And we look forward to seeing you in many more. I'll let you get back to your fans now. Thanks."

Pearl nodded and turned toward a huge crowd. They were all chanting, "Pearl! Pearl!"

One screaming fan even broke through the crowd and tried to hug Pearl. Then the fan began shaking Pearl's shoulders.

"What are you doing?" Pearl cried. "Stop that right now!"

"Pearl! Pearl! Wake up, my little pupfish!"

Pearl's eyes popped open. She wasn't surrounded by screaming fans. Instead she was in her bed, surrounded by a curtain of daisy coral, and the person shaking her shoulders was her mother!

"Pearl, you must have been having a dream. It's time for school."

Pearl hugged her mother. "I dreamed I was a famous meractress," she explained. "A real star of the sea!"

"You are always a sea star to me!" Mrs. Swamp said, kissing the top of Pearl's head. "Now, come to breakfast. The mercook made water-flea waffles this morning."

Pearl jumped up and ran a Venus comb through her hair. Her dream had felt so real: the screaming fans, the flowers, and the beautiful costumes on the glittering stage. Pearl's greatest wish was to become a star someday—and that day couldn't come soon enough!

2

Angelfish Molie

PEARL YAWNED AS SHE POURED sandweed syrup on her water-flea waffles. She took a big bite and looked at her father. Mr. Swamp was reading the newsweed while sipping his favorite copepod coffee. Usually Pearl didn't read the *Trident City Tide* because she found most of its news stories quite dull. But this time she squealed when she saw the back of her father's kelp.

"Oh my Neptune!" Pearl shouted. "Angelfish Molie is coming to Trident City!"

Mr. Swamp was so startled by Pearl's shout that he spilled coffee all over his gold-and-black-striped tail. "What are you yelling about so early in the morning?" he asked, using his kelp napkin to wipe up the mess.

"You're always telling me I should keep up with the local news, so I read the back of the *Trident City Tide*." Pearl pointed to an article that said that Angelfish Molie, the most famous meractress in all the ocean, would be starring in *Gone with the Tide* at the Grand Banks Theater. And the play was opening Tuesday night—tomorrow evening!

"Please, Daddy," Pearl begged. "Can you take me to see her?" Dreaming about being famous was fun, but actually seeing a star perform in person would be totally wavy.

Mr. Swamp nodded. "I'll see if I can get tickets."

Pearl threw herself at her father and gave him a big hug, overturning her water-flea waffles in the process.

"I can't wait to tell Wanda!" Pearl shrieked. "This is the most exciting thing that has ever happened in the history of Trident City!"

Pearl dressed for school in record time and soared through the water to Trident Academy. She found her best friend, Wanda Slug, waiting for her in the school's huge front entrance hall.

"Pearl!" Wanda called. "I have wonderful news!"

"Is it about Angelfish Molie?" Pearl asked.

Wanda shook her head. "No, this is much better."

Pearl couldn't imagine anything being more wonderful than getting to see the most famous meractress in the ocean.

"What's better than Angelfish Molie?" Pearl demanded.

"This!" Wanda exclaimed, pointing to a sign hanging nearby.

Pearl cheered when she read the announcement.

TRIDENT ACADEMY'S THIRD-GRADE CLASS PROUDLY PRESENTS

The Little Human

A PLAY IN TWO ACTS

TRYOUTS WEDNESDAY IN FINN AUDITORIUM!

QUESTIONS? SEE MRS. J. KARP.

3

Sea Star

PEARL BURST INTO HER THIRD-grade classroom. "Mrs. Karp, is it true? Are we really putting on a play?"

Mrs. Karp raised one green eyebrow before smiling at Pearl and her other students. "Yes, every year the third grade puts on a theatrical performance for friends, family, and the rest of Trident Academy. This year's play is *The Little Human*. It's a story that many of you may know about a human, a shark, and a rather scary witch. Tryouts are Wednesday after school."

Pearl, Wanda, and several other mergirls squealed with delight.

A boy named Rocky Ridge groaned. "We don't have to try out, do we?"

Mrs. Karp shook her head. "Of course not, but I hope you will. We need lots of meractors and meractresses and a strong stage crew in order for our show to be a success. The play could not go on without people building and painting the backgrounds, which are called sets. We even need someone to pull the seaweed curtain open. Each part in a play is important!"

"It might be fun," a merboy named Adam said.

Echo Reef nodded. "I love anything to do with humans. And *The Little Human* is one of my favorite stories. I'm definitely trying out. What about you, Shelly?"

Shelly Siren shrugged. "Maybe." She was usually more interested in sports than performing.

Pearl didn't say a word. She just smiled. Today was turning out to be a fabulous day. After all, she'd dreamed of being a star, Angelfish Molie was coming to town, and now Pearl was going to be in a real play.

Of course, Pearl just knew she'd get the lead role of the human girl in *The Little Human*! No one else in the third grade was as good an actress as Pearl. She imagined the costume she would wear as the audience cheered for her. She wondered what kind of sea flowers they'd throw at her feet. She was so busy daydreaming that she barely heard Mrs. Karp asking her a question.

"Pearl?" Mrs. Karp said. "Can you name a sea creature that can regrow an arm?"

Pearl just looked at her teacher. Mrs. Karp tapped her chin with her white tail while she waited for Pearl's answer. Pearl didn't know, so she said the first animal that came to her mind.

"A zebra shark?" she guessed. Pearl shuddered as she said this. She hated sharks!

Rocky laughed out loud. "Sharks don't have arms!"

Mrs. Karp frowned at Rocky. "Mr. Ridge, don't be rude," she told him. "Does anyone else know the answer?"

The smallest girl in the class, Kiki Coral, raised her hand slowly. "Are you talking about sea stars?"

Mrs. Karp nodded. "Yes, Kiki, that's correct."

"What's a sea star?" Shelly asked.

"Most merpeople know sea stars by their other name, starfish," Mrs. Karp explained. "But since they are not actually fish, 'sea star' is the correct name."

"Can they really grow back their arms?" Wanda asked.

Mrs. Karp smiled. "Yes, they are amazing little creatures. They usually have five arms, but some have up to twenty!"

"I'd love to have twenty arms," Rocky said. "I'd be the most famous Shell Wars player in the ocean!" Shell Wars was a sport that was played by whacking a seashell with whale bones.

Mrs. Karp continued talking about sea stars, but Pearl could only think about one kind of star: herself! She was back to imagining being onstage in *The Little Human*.

Pearl's dream was coming true! She was going to be a famous merstar—and nothing was going to stand in her way.

4

Trip to the Hotel

LATER THAT DAY, PEARL'S stomach growled as she scooped up an extra-big helping of her favorite school lunch, black-lip oyster and sablefish stew.

"Ooh, and there's white sea whip pudding for dessert," she said with a giggle.

"This day keeps getting better and better."

Pearl even decided to get some herbed lichen fruit from the fruit bar. She didn't normally like fruit, but her mother loved for her to eat healthy food. Since she was having such a great day, she figured, why not?

Echo, Shelly, and Kiki floated in front of the fruit bar. Pearl started to ask them to get out of her way, but then she heard Echo say, "Let's go to the Trident Plaza Hotel after school. Maybe my mom will know where we can get a peek at Angelfish Molie!"

Pearl gasped. She knew that Echo's mother was the director of the Conservatory for the Preservation of Sea Horses and Swordfish, which was located inside the hotel. And the Grand Banks Theater, where Angelfish was performing, was in the hotel too. Would Angelfish really be swimming around between rehearsals?

"I'm in," Shelly said.

"Me too," Kiki added. "I've never seen a real live theater star before."

"Can I come?" Pearl asked Echo. "Angelfish Molie is my favorite mer-actress!"

"Sure," Echo said. "Meet us in the front hall after school. We'll leave from there."

After that, Pearl couldn't wait for school to be over. She was so glad she didn't have Tail Flippers practice that afternoon. Pearl had been excited when she had made Trident Academy's flipping team earlier in the year, but Coach Barnacle was very strict about missing practice.

When the last conch shell sounded, Pearl was the first student at the school's door. She didn't even glance at the colorful carvings of merpeople or the sparkling chandelier that were her favorite parts of the front hallway. She played with her pearl necklace and tapped her gold tail impatiently as she waited for Echo, Shelly, and Kiki to arrive.

"Hi, Pearl," Wanda said, swimming up beside her. Other merkids floated past them on their way home or to after-school activities. "What are you doing?"

Pearl sighed. "I'm going to the Trident Plaza Hotel to try to see Angelfish Molie.

That is, if Echo, Shelly, and Kiki ever get here." Pearl didn't think she could wait another mersecond.

"No wavy way!" Wanda exclaimed. "Can I come too?"

"Sure," Echo said as she swam up beside the girls. Kiki and Shelly floated behind her.

"Finally you're here!" Pearl said, rolling her eyes. "Now let's go!"

"Shake your tail!" Echo laughed, and the mergirls zoomed across town to the Trident Plaza Hotel.

As they swam through the hotel's grand doors, Pearl scanned the polished green marble floors and shining brass walls of the lobby, but she didn't see Angelfish anywhere. Pearl groaned when she noticed the creepy shark statue in front of the Conservatory for the Preservation of Sea Horses and Swordfish. That statue had always scared her.

Echo floated into the conservatory but came out a few minutes later, shaking her head. "My mom says that she hasn't seen Angelfish anywhere."

Just then Pearl noticed something that made her fins spin. It was her teacher, Mrs. Karp. And she was hugging Angelfish Molie!

5

JoJo

THE OTHER MERGIRLS SAW Mrs. Karp too.

"Sweet seaweed!" Echo shrieked. "How does Mrs. Karp know Angelfish Molie?"

"I don't know," Pearl said, "but we need to find out." Her heart pounded in her chest. She was finally going to meet her favorite star!

Wanda shook her head. "I don't think we should swim over there. It's rude to interrupt."

Kiki nodded. "That's true."

The five girls looked at one another. Pearl couldn't believe they were going to pass up this chance. "Well, *I* want to interrupt," she said.

With that, Pearl flipped her tail and, fast as a sailfish, swam up to Mrs. Karp. The other girls quietly followed Pearl.

"Look who's here!" Mrs. Karp said with a smile. "Angelfish, these are some of my students from Trident Academy. Mergirls, meet Angelfish Molie."

Echo, Shelly, Kiki, and Wanda floated with their mouths and eyes wide open. Kiki squeaked out a tiny, "Nice to meet you."

Pearl reached out to shake Angelfish Molie's hand. She couldn't believe she was actually going to touch Angelfish! But the star didn't shake Pearl's hand. Instead she grabbed Pearl and gave her a big hug! Then she hugged each of the other mergirls.

"I am so happy to meet some of JoJo's students," said Angelfish. "Did she tell you that we're old friends?"

Mrs. Karp's name was JoJo? Pearl hid a smile behind her hand.

The other mergirls shook their heads in surprise, and Angelfish laughed. "Well, JoJo," she said, turning to Mrs. Karp.

"You always were good at keeping secrets."

"Did JoJo—I mean Mrs. Karp—tell you that we are putting on a play at our school?" Pearl asked.

"A play?" Angelfish exclaimed. "Fin-tastic!"

Pearl couldn't help noticing that dozens of people had stopped to stare at their little group. They probably weren't used to seeing a famous merstar in Trident City. Pearl smiled and flipped her long blond ponytail. She loved being the center of attention.

Mrs. Karp nodded. "Yes, we are holding tryouts on Wednesday for *The Little Human*."

"That's one of my favorites," Angelfish said, clapping her hands. "Actually, I have some free time Wednesday afternoon. I'd love to help."

Echo and Wanda gasped.

"We'd be honored to have you," Mrs. Karp said.

"Well, I'd better go prepare for my own play," Angelfish told them. "I hope you'll come to see me perform tomorrow night." She pulled a small stack of tickets from her shell

purse and passed one to each mergirl and to Mrs. Karp.

"Thank you, Miss Molie, but I don't know if I should take one," Pearl explained. "My father was going to try to get tickets today."

Angelfish shook her head. "Oh honey, this show has been sold out for weeks. Plus, these are front-row seats. Take one and you mergirls can all sit together."

"Thank you," the mergirls said in unison.

Angelfish wiggled away through the lobby. Everyone looked at her. Some pointed and whispered to their merfriends, while others just drifted and stared in awe.

Pearl smiled. She knew that when she was famous, merfolk would look at her that way too.

"I've never seen a play at the Grand Banks Theater before," Wanda squealed.

Mrs. Karp smiled and said in her teacher voice, "Well, I'm glad you merladies are excited about tomorrow's performance, but now you need to go home and do tonight's homework."

"Let's go!" Kiki urged her friends.

But as Pearl swam home, schoolwork was the last thing on her mind. First, she had to decide what to wear to the theater. Maybe her mother would take her shopping for a new outfit. After all, it wasn't every day that she got to see Angelfish Molie in a play!

Yes, this was definitely the best day ever, but Pearl knew that getting to see Angelfish perform in person would make tomorrow even better!

Black Ties and Pearls

"I CAN'T BELIEVE WE'RE ACTUALLY here," Pearl told Shelly.

The following night the two girls were with Echo, Kiki, Wanda, and Mrs. Karp in the huge Grand Banks Theater at the Trident Plaza Hotel. Bioluminescent plankton formed sparkling pictures on the walls as an orchestra played quietly. Whenever the music changed, the plankton rearranged to become a totally new picture. It happened so quickly that it looked like the pictures themselves were moving.

Elegant merpeople dressed in black ties and pearls filled the shell-back seats, chatting with one another or watching the moving pictures. Pearl wore her pearl necklace and her very best pink sparkly top, but she wasn't sure it was fancy enough. Some elderly merwomen even wore long white gloves and huge diamond rings!

"How did you meet Angelfish Molie?" Echo asked Mrs. Karp.

"I used to work for her," Mrs. Karp explained.

"You worked for Angelfish Molie?" Pearl asked. She couldn't imagine why a teacher would work for an actress!

"Yes," Mrs. Karp answered slowly. "You could say I was her . . . guard."

Pearl was shocked. Before she could ask another question, Mrs. Karp put her finger to her lips. "Shhh. The show is about to start."

The seaweed curtain went up, and out came Angelfish in the most gorgeous costume Pearl had ever seen. Her skirt was made of glowing comb jellies, and her top was covered with rubies and emeralds that glittered in the low stage lights. Soon the whole audience was laughing at Angelfish's jokes.

Pearl couldn't tear her eyes away from the stage, especially when Angelfish's character fell in love with a handsome meractor. It was so romantic! Pearl almost fainted when he hugged Angelfish tightly and told her he loved her.

Echo giggled at that moment, and Pearl felt like tail-kicking her. Didn't Echo know this was a serious part?

It was a long play—more than two merhours—but Pearl didn't mind. It could have been twice as long and she still would have loved it. After the curtain fell, the audience clapped and whistled. It was just like in Pearl's dream—only

this time she wasn't the one on stage.

The mergirls and Mrs. Karp left the theater and stepped into the Plaza Hotel's lobby. Shiny light gleamed off the brass walls and polished floors. Everything sparkled! But Pearl's eyes twinkled from her excitement.

"Well, merladies, what did you think?" Mrs. Karp asked.

"It was great," Shelly said.

"Mervelous," Kiki agreed.

"Splash-errific," Echo said with a nod.

"Shelltacular." Wanda sighed.

Mrs. Karp looked at Pearl. "Pearl, you're so quiet. Didn't you enjoy the play?"

Pearl was so inspired she could hardly speak, but she managed to whisper, "Oh,

Mrs. Karp. It was the most wonderful night ever. Thank you so much for introducing us to Miss Molie."

Mrs. Karp smiled. "You'll have to remember to thank Angelfish for the tickets tomorrow at tryouts."

"I will!" Pearl said.

Now she was sure that more than anything she wanted to be exactly like Angelfish Molie. Pearl wanted to be a star. And tomorrow she would get her chance when Angelfish cast her as the little human!

Play Time

THE NEXT DAY AT SCHOOL, Angelfish's performance at the Grand Banks was all Pearl could think about.

"Your next project," Mrs. Karp said, "is to choose two sea stars and compare and contrast their characteristics."

"What does compare and contrast mean?" Rocky blurted.

Mrs. Karp smiled. "I'm glad you asked. Let me explain."

Pearl tried to pay attention to her teacher—after all, some starfish, or sea stars, were kind of cute—but she was too excited! Pearl just knew that Angelfish would choose her to be the star of the play. Pearl was surprised that she even had to try out. After all, no one else in the third grade wanted the part of the little human as badly as she did. And no one deserved it as much as Pearl!

In fact, Pearl was sure Angelfish would be so impressed that she'd want to be friends. Maybe they could practice their lines together, or go shopping for new jewels and sparkling costumes.

Finally, after what seemed like the longest day in merhistory, the last conch shell sounded. Pearl shot out of her desk and was the first to enter her school's Finn Auditorium.

But when she arrived, the horrible shark statue from the lobby of the Trident Plaza Hotel was sitting right in the middle of the stage!

Pearl's heart pounded with fear. She couldn't forget the time a great white shark had chased her into Trident Academy. Pearl had almost been eaten! After that, she had hoped never to see a shark—even a statue—at school ever again.

"What is that doing here?" Pearl screeched.

To Pearl's surprise, Angelfish Molie swam over to her. "Oh, that was my idea. I borrowed it from the hotel because I thought it would be the perfect prop for your play. There is a scene where the little human has to flee from a shark."

Though she was happy to see Angelfish, Pearl shuddered. She really disliked sharks and everything about them. And she'd been scared of that statue ever since she'd been a little fry.

After the rest of the third graders and their teacher had floated into the auditorium, Mrs. Karp clapped her hands. "All right," she said. "Everyone please swim up to the stage and select a script to read from. Each script is for a different part in the play, but there are enough to go around."

Pearl hated to go near the statue, but she closed her eyes and grabbed a script. She darted away from the shark as quickly as she could.

"Let's begin with the merboys," Angelfish announced. "Everyone with a prince script, sit over here."

Pearl looked down at her script. "Oh no!" she cried, dashing toward her teacher. She had been so scared of the statue that she had accidentally picked up the script for the evil witch.

"Mrs. Karp," Pearl said, tapping her teacher on the shoulder. "There's been a terrible mistake! I grabbed the wrong script. I don't want to try out for the witch. I want to play the part of the human girl."

"I'm afraid there aren't any of those left," Mrs. Karp told her. "But don't worry. Angelfish and I will choose the best merstudent for each part, no matter what you read."

"You mean I'll still be the star?" Pearl asked.

"Everyone is a star in this play, but you could certainly get any part, no matter which script you have," Mrs. Karp explained.

Just then, Wanda shrieked, "ARGH! Shark!"

Pearl was glad someone else was afraid of the shark statue. But Wanda wasn't looking at the statue. Instead she pointed to a scary-looking fin moving across the back of the auditorium! Pearl's heart thumped in her chest. Was there a shark loose in Trident Academy?

Mrs. Karp smacked her tail on the auditorium floor. "Rocky Ridge, get out from behind those seats immediately!"

Rocky floated into the aisle with a grin on his face and a fake shark fin on his head. "But Mrs. Karp, I want to try out for the part of the shark," he said.

Wanda shook her finger at Rocky. "You scared the seaweed out of me!"

"Don't get your tail in a knot," Rocky told her. "I was just kidding around."

"All right, let's get busy," Mrs. Karp said, turning everyone's attention away from Rocky and Wanda.

Pearl thought tryouts went very well, in spite of the horrible statue. Even though she had to read the part of the witch, she still wanted to do a good job. So she made the witch sound very evil, indeed! She figured that stars always do their best—even when they're reading for the wrong part.

"Pearl, you were wonderful," Wanda told her.

"So were you!" Pearl told her best friend—and she meant it. Wanda had read for the part of the little human, and she was so good that Pearl thought for a moment that she really *was* the little human. Wanda was probably the finest actress in the whole third grade—besides Pearl, of course. Pearl was fins and tail above everyone else.

So at the end of the afternoon, when Angelfish announced the parts, Pearl couldn't believe her ears.

Stolen Dreams

"THE WITCH?" PEARL SHOOK her head. Maybe she'd misheard. She checked to make sure she didn't have sand in her ears.

"Yes." Angelfish nodded and looked at her rock pad. "Pearl Swamp will play the part of the witch."

"But I . . ." Pearl was so upset that she could barely speak.

Angelfish smiled. "You'll make a great witch."

Rocky snickered. "She's a witch all right."

One stern glance from Mrs. Karp silenced Rocky, and Angelfish continued reading off the names of which merstudent got which part.

Tears filled Pearl's eyes as she choked back a sob. She was afraid she would start crying at any moment. How could she have been chosen to be the stinky old witch? She wanted to be the star. She *should* be the star! Angelfish had obviously made a mistake.

"Adam Pelagic will play the part of the prince," Angelfish announced. He smiled a goofy smile as Rocky patted him on the shoulder.

"Rocky will be King Neptune. Echo, Kiki, and Shelly will play the sisters. Morgan will be the mother. And, finally, the part of the little human will be played by . . ."

Pearl held her breath. Surely Angelfish would call her name now. Pearl just *had* to be the little human!

"Wanda Slug!"

Several mergirls clapped, but Pearl

gasped. Wanda was supposed to be Pearl's best friend! How could Wanda do this to her?

"Thank you, everyone, for trying out," Mrs. Karp said. "We'll start rehearsing tomorrow after school. Please take your scripts home so you can study your lines. And don't forget your sea star homework!"

Pearl could barely move. It all felt like a bad dream!

Wanda floated over with a big smile on her face. "Pearl! I'm so excited that we'll be in the play together. Can you believe I got the part of the little human?"

"Yes, it *is* hard to believe," Pearl muttered.

"It's so exciting!" Wanda giggled. "I've

always wanted to be in a play, but I never thought it would actually happen to me. *The Little Human* is my favorite story ever."

Pearl knew she should be happy for Wanda. Pearl should pat her friend on the back and hug her. But she just couldn't bring herself to do it.

Instead Pearl could do only one thing. "I have to go start my homework," she blurted.

She swam away from the tryouts and the awful shark statue. She swam away from her hopes of being a star.

If yesterday had been the best day ever, today was the worst. Not only had she lost her dream, but her best friend had stolen it from her!

9
Witch Switch

NORMALLY, PEARL LOVED Trident Academy's lunch special of star puffer fish stew, but the day after tryouts, she just pushed it around her shell bowl. Her stomach twisted as she listened to Wanda talk about the play.

"I studied my lines almost all night," Wanda told the other mergirls at their table, "but there are so many! I just don't know how I'm going to learn them all."

"I can help you practice," Morgan offered.

Pearl smiled as she looked up from her stew. That was it! She knew Wanda hated memorizing things.

"Wanda," Pearl said slowly. "If the little human part has too many lines, we could switch. You could be the witch instead."

Every mergirl at the table stared at Pearl. Wanda shook her head. "I *do* want to be the little human. I just meant it will be hard to learn all those lines."

"But the witch part is much easier," Pearl insisted. "I want to help you by playing the harder part."

"Pearl, are you trying to take Wanda's part?" Morgan asked in a shocked voice.

"Well, *I* deserve to be the little human, not Wanda!" Pearl cried. "If she was really my friend, she'd switch with me!" Pearl slapped her hand over her mouth. She couldn't believe she'd actually said it out loud, even though it was true.

Just then Echo glided by with her lunch tray. "Pearl!" she said. "How could you say that?"

Wanda put her hand on Pearl's shoulder. "I didn't know being the little human meant so much to you."

"Well, it does!" Pearl snapped. "I was supposed to be the star."

"I guess I *could* switch parts with you," Wanda said softly.

Pearl looked at her best friend. She noticed that Wanda had a tear in the corner of one eye. Even though she felt bad for Wanda, Pearl couldn't help being excited, too. If Wanda really did give up her part, Pearl's dream would come true. She could be the star after all!

That was why even Pearl was shocked by what came out of her own mouth.

"No, you should be the little human," Pearl said. "You were picked tails down."

"Are you sure?" Wanda asked, wiping tears from her eyes.

Pearl wanted to yell, *No!* But she didn't. Instead she nodded and said, "Yes, I'm sure. Don't worry. You'll be great."

She bit her lip. Now it was Pearl's turn to cry. Would her sea star dreams ever come true?

10
Quitting Time

"WHY DIDN'T I LET HER switch with me?" Pearl muttered to herself that afternoon at play practice.

Wanda and a group of mergirls clustered at a corner of the stage, giggling and practicing their lines. Pearl sighed.

She didn't think she could stand listening to that every day. It was just too painful to watch her best friend practice the part Pearl had wanted.

Suddenly she smiled. She didn't have to listen to them. She could just quit.

Once Pearl had made up her mind, she didn't waste a mersecond. She soared over to Mrs. Karp and announced, "I am quitting the play."

Mrs. Karp's eyes grew wide with surprise. "But I thought you loved plays."

"I do—er—I did," Pearl sputtered. "But actually being in a play isn't as much fun as I thought it would be." She didn't add that it would have been fun if she'd been chosen to play the little human.

Mrs. Karp frowned at Pearl. "I'm sorry to hear that."

After she handed Mrs. Karp her script, Pearl took one last look at the stage and at the scary statue of the shark. She wanted to kick that shark in the fin! After all, if she hadn't been scared of the statue, she would have picked up the right script. Then she would have been chosen to be the little human instead of Wanda. Pearl fought back tears as she hurried out of the auditorium. Mrs. Karp had said the script didn't matter, but obviously it had.

Pearl was almost to the front door of Trident Academy when she felt a tug on her gold tail. She swirled around to snap at whoever had grabbed her, but she stopped short when she saw who it was.

"Angelfish!" Pearl gasped. "I mean, Miss Molie."

As Angelfish smiled, Pearl could see why she was a star. Her smile was so big it seemed to light up the entire front hallway of the school.

"Sorry to tug on your tail," Angelfish said. "I came by to help JoJo again this afternoon, and she told me that you quit the play."

Pearl nodded. "I did."

"That's the problem," Angelfish told her. "I don't think you should."

Pearl couldn't help herself. Something about Angelfish and her big smile made

Pearl want to tell her everything. "But I wanted to be the star," she blurted. "I wanted to be the little human so badly."

"I know. JoJo was going to choose you for that part, but I talked her out of it," Angelfish told her.

Pearl stared at Angelfish in horror. "Why would you do that to me?" Pearl said in shock.

That Sea Star Spark

"LET'S TALK," ANGELFISH SAID. She pulled Pearl over to a small rock table and chairs.

Pearl didn't want to listen to Angelfish. How could Pearl ever have admired the meractress? She might be a great star, but she was also just plain mean.

As if she could read Pearl's mind, Angelfish patted her on the arm and said, "I didn't do it to be cruel. I did it to help you."

Pearl pulled her arm away. She longed to swim home and never come back to Trident Academy again.

"Let me explain," Angelfish began. "I wanted you to play the part of the witch because it's such an important part."

"It is?" Pearl asked.

Angelfish nodded. "The evil roles are often the biggest ones. Without them, most plays would be a little dull."

Angelfish went on, "Plus, just between us mergirls, I knew it would be the most exciting part to play. Much more fun than the human girl."

"Fun?" Pearl repeated. What was Angelfish talking about?

"Oh yes," Angelfish said with her huge smile. "The evil characters are always more enjoyable to play than the sweet ones."

"They are?" Pearl asked.

Angelfish nodded. "Mean characters are a blast. You wouldn't want to be that way in real life, but it's so fun to pretend."

"But I wanted to be the star," Pearl said sadly.

Angelfish shook her head. "But being a star isn't the best part of acting. The best part is being onstage."

Then she leaned in to whisper, "Pearl, I think you have the makings of a fin-tastic actress. You have that sea star spark. And the part of the witch needs that spark!"

Pearl gasped. Angelfish thought she had a spark? A sea star spark?

"Please come back to the play and see if I'm right," Angelfish said.

Now Pearl didn't know what to think. If Angelfish was telling the truth, then Pearl would have more fun than anyone in the school play—even Wanda!

"Please, Pearl?" Angelfish asked again. "Just give it a try."

"All right," Pearl said slowly.

She took a deep gulp of water and swam back into the auditorium. After Angelfish had a quick word with Mrs. Karp, Pearl dived right into rehearsals.

She looked at her script and closed her eyes. When she opened them again, she screamed at Wanda, "You will never escape from me!"

Wanda was so startled by Pearl's performance that she forgot her next line.

Pearl had to whisper it under her breath.

As they continued to rehearse, Pearl realized that Angelfish had been right after all. It *was* fun to play the mean character. Wanda got to say a lot of sweet lines, but Pearl was able to scream, slap her tail, and make terrible faces. It was totally wavy!

After practice, Wanda said, "Pearl, you are an amazing actress!"

"Thanks. You make a good little human," Pearl said with a smile.

12
The Curtain Falls

THE WEEKS OF REHEARSALS seemed to fly by. When the night for the play finally arrived, Pearl was almost sad. She was excited to perform in front of a real audience, but she'd loved practicing with her class, too. Every merstudent had something special to add. When Adam was so nervous he accidentally sang his line, Mrs. Karp had liked it so much she had him sing a whole song. Pearl was surprised at how nice his voice was. Morgan had everyone laughing at the funny voice she used for the mother. Pearl was beginning to see what Mrs. Karp meant about how each part was important.

As the curtain opened and Pearl saw all the parents and students sitting in front of her, she got a little scared. And then the unthinkable happened: she forgot her most important line!

Luckily, Wanda remembered.

"You'll never escape," Wanda whispered.

Pearl smiled. But it wasn't a sweet smile. It was the smile of an evil villain!

"You will never escape from me!" Pearl screamed at Wanda.

Wanda fell into a pile of seaweed and cried while Pearl battled Rocky as King Neptune. When it was time for the witch to die, Pearl fell to the stage with a loud shriek. Everyone clapped as the curtains closed.

Rocky grinned. "You were awesome, Pearl!" he said.

Pearl couldn't believe Rocky had said something nice to her. Usually, he just teased her. "Thanks," she said. "You were pretty good too."

But what *really* made Pearl feel great was seeing Angelfish Molie backstage after the show.

"I can't believe you came to see us perform!" Pearl said. She had read that Angelfish had been performing *Gone with the Tide* in the nearby city of Poseidon.

Angelfish gave Pearl a huge hug.

"I wouldn't have missed it for anything. And you stole the show!" Angelfish said. "But more importantly, did you have a good time?"

"The best," Pearl admitted. Then she realized that, though she *had* loved when everyone clapped for her, she'd enjoyed pretending with her classmates most of all.

Angelfish smiled. "I knew you'd adore it." She swam off to congratulate the rest of the cast on their great performance.

Wanda splashed over to Pearl. "I'm glad that's over," Wanda whispered.

"Didn't you like being the little human?" Pearl asked.

"Are you kidding?" Wanda said. "I was scared to death of performing in front of all those merfolk. Weren't you?"

Pearl shook her head. It was the most fun she'd ever had.

She did feel bad about one thing. "Wanda, I'm sorry I tried to get you to switch parts. It wasn't very nice of me."

"That's okay. Maybe I should have switched," Wanda said. "You were the real star of the play."

"Me?" Pearl asked.

"Yes, you," Wanda said with a smile.

Pearl gave her friend a hug. "I couldn't have done it without you helping me with my line! We were *both* stars!"

Wanda giggled. "Just like Angelfish Molie."

Pearl laughed. "Tails down!" she said. In her mind she could still hear the cheers of the crowd. She couldn't wait to get onstage again!

Class Compare-and-Contrast Projects

★ ★ ★

H CHART

By Shelly Siren

The Mosaic Sea Star and the Goosefoot Sea Star

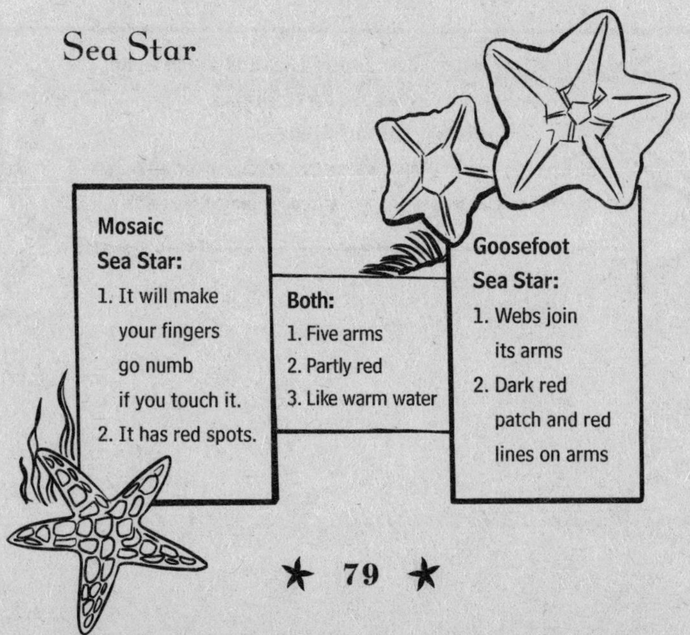

ALIKE AND DIFFERENT CHART

By Echo Reef

The Icon Star and the Seven-Armed Sea Star

How the Icon Star and the Seven-Armed Sea Star Are Alike:

Long, thin arms

Live in the ocean

How the Icon Star and the Seven-Armed Sea Star Are Different:

The seven-armed sea star has seven arms.

The icon star has five arms.

The icon star lives in deeper waters than the seven-armed sea star.

The icon star has a pretty pattern, and the seven-armed sea star is one color.

VENN DIAGRAM

By Rocky Ridge

The Sunflower Sea Star and the Basket Star

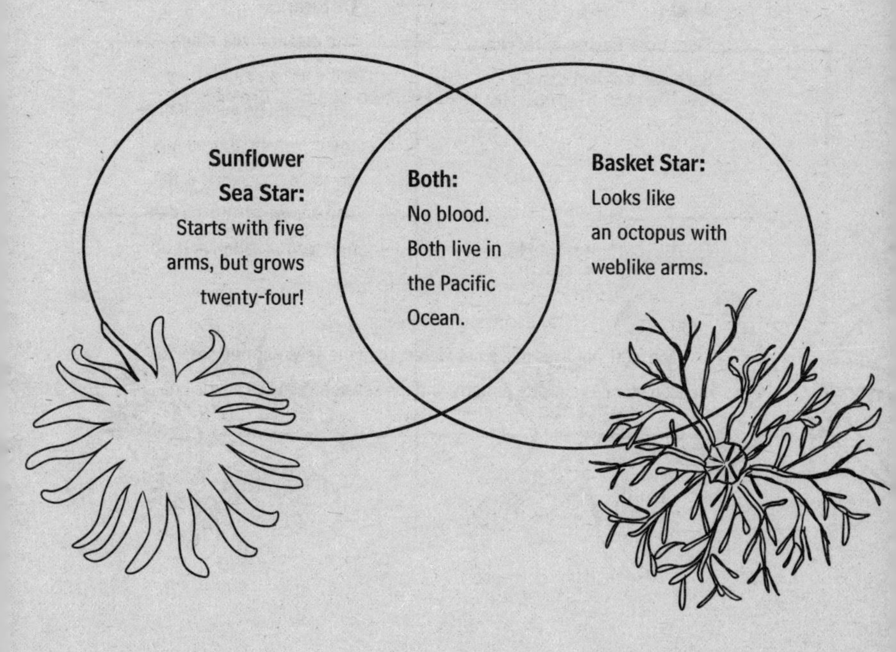

T CHART

By Kiki Coral

The Cushion Sea Star and the Crown-of-Thorns Sea Star

Alike:	**Different:**
They both live on coral reefs. Both will eat live coral.	The cushion sea star's arms are so small they can hardly be seen, while the crown-of-thorns has up to twenty spiny arms. The crown-of-thorns can hurt you if you pick it up.

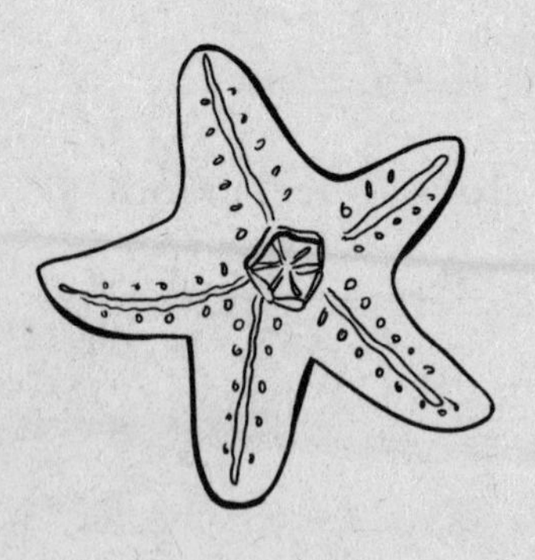

COMPARE-AND-CONTRAST ESSAY

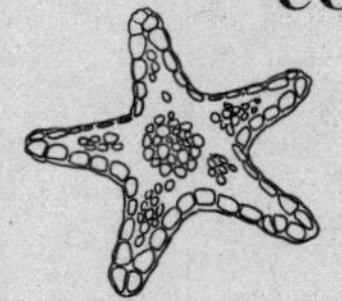

By Pearl Swamp

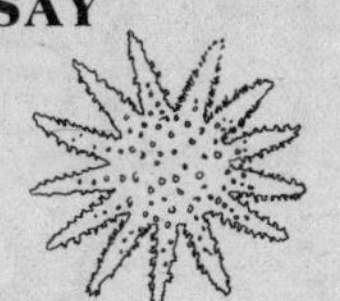

The Sun Star and the Biscuit Sea Star

Both are kind of ugly if you ask me, but I do like their names. The sun star has fourteen arms, while the biscuit sea star is more normal and has five. The sun star is one of the larger sea stars, and the biscuit is one of the smaller. It's about the size of a biscuit.

They are both sea stars, but I'm not sure why. They look different, but they do both have arms and a middle section. They use seawater instead of blood, which is really weird.

REFRAIN:

Let the water roar 

Deep down we're swimming along

Twirling, swirling, singing the mermaid song.

VERSE 1:

Shelly flips her tail

Racing, diving, chasing a whale

Twirling, swirling, singing the mermaid song.

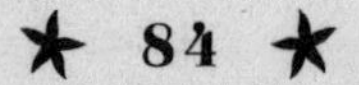

VERSE 2:

Pearl likes to shine

Oh my Neptune, she looks so fine

Twirling, swirling, singing the mermaid song.

VERSE 3:

Shining Echo flips her tail

Backward and forward without fail

Twirling, swirling, singing the mermaid song.

VERSE 4:

Amazing Kiki

Far from home and floating so free

Twirling, swirling, singing the mermaid song

Author's Note

I'M NOT SURE WHY, BUT MY ELEMENTARY school never put on a single play. I wish they had, because it would have been great fun. So when I got to high school, I never even dreamed of trying out. Maybe I was afraid, or maybe I thought that was for other people who were somehow better than me. Now I wish I'd been brave enough to try. My daughter was one of those courageous kids who tried out for her high school plays. She also helped out with the stage crew. She had great fun, and I loved watching her perform. She didn't have the lead parts, but she was my star. She still is!

I hope if you get the chance to be in a school play, you will give it a try. You might just have the time of your life.

Your mermaid friend,
Debbie Dadey

ANGELFISH: The queen angelfish is one of the most colorful reef fish in the Caribbean. This thin blue-and-yellow fish nibbles on sponges, its main food source.

BASKET STAR: This sea star can live to be thirty-five years old and looks like a funny baby octopus.

BISCUIT SEA STAR: This sea star is bright orange-red and lives around Australia.

BLACK-LIP OYSTER: The black-lip pearl

oyster begins life as a male before changing into a female two or three years later. It is famous because it sometimes creates prized black pearls.

COMB JELLY: The predatory comb jelly swims by moving eight rows of cilia combs that shimmer with iridescent colors. It has a slightly flattened pear shape.

CONCH: The queen conch is a mollusk that has been used for food and bait by humans. This has caused a decrease in the conch population. It is illegal to take a queen conch from the water in Florida. It has a large spiral shell that is sold in gift shops in some countries.

COPEPOD: This tiny creature makes up most of the total zooplankton population.

Plankton is a food source for many marine animals.

CROWN-OF-THORNS: This sea star has up to twenty arms and can give you a painful wound if you pick it up.

CUSHION SEA STAR: This sea star looks like a blob. Its arms are so short, they can barely be seen. Tiny shrimp live on the cushion star.

DAISY CORAL: The daisy coral looks very much like a daisy flower.

GOOSE FOOT SEA STAR: This sea star's body really does resemble a webbed foot.

GREAT WHITE SHARK: The great white shark has a reputation for being the most dangerous shark in the ocean. Its natural food includes fish, seals, and even penguins.

ICON STAR: Each of these sea stars has a unique pattern of plates that line the edge of its arms and body.

JELLYFISH: Deep-sea jellyfish are shaped liked a ballet tutu. This jellyfish can actually squirt out a glowing substance to confuse its enemies.

KELP: Giant kelp is the biggest of all seaweed.

LAMPERN: The lampern is also known as the river lamprey. Adult lamperns never get very far from the coast.

LICHEN: Sea ivory is a type of gray lichen that often grows on vertical rock faces.

MOSAIC SEA STAR: This sea star is so bright that you might want to pick it up. But don't touch it; it will cause your hands to go numb!

OCTOPUS: The giant octopus is very smart. A mother will guard her eggs for eight months until they hatch.

ORANGE SEA PEN: This creature looks surprisingly like an old-fashioned quill pen.

PIDDOCK: The common piddock can squirt out a glowing blue liquid when it is afraid.

PUPFISH: This very small fish is usually only one to two inches long—shorter than your finger!

SABLEFISH: Sablefish breed slowly. It takes fourteen years to replace one that is caught.

SAILFISH: The Atlantic sailfish has a long upper jaw like a swordfish. The sailfish has a huge sail-like dorsal fin, which it folds away for fast swimming.

SANDWEED: This type of seaweed forms a spongy mat that often covers rocks near the shore.

SEA HORSE: Sea horses do look a lot like horses, except that sea horses do not have legs and are tiny in comparison.

SEA LAVENDER: Sea lavender grows along marshy shorelines. It blooms in the summer with purple or lavender blooms.

SEA STAR: Commonly known as starfish, this star-shaped creature lives on the ocean floor. Its mouth is on its underside, and it has five or more arms.

SEAWEED: There are over six thousand types of seaweed. One type of red seaweed that grows near shores is called Irish Moss.

SEVEN-ARMED SEA STAR: This sea star's

seven arms are lined with small white spines that help it to hide in small rocks.

STAR PUFFER FISH: This is a giant among puffer fish. It has black-spotted skin that is covered with prickles, and it grows to be about four feet long. If it is scared, it swallows water and puffs up to appear much larger.

SUNFLOWER SEA STAR: This sea star looks like a mop!

SUN STAR: This sea star has fourteen arms and will eat other sea stars.

SWORDFISH: The swordfish uses its sharp, pointed bill for hunting and protection.

VENUS COMB: This snail has a shell that looks like a two-sided comb.

WATERFLEA: The tiny water flea has a large

eye and feathery swimming appendages.

WHITE SEA WHIP: Sea whips are similar to sea fans, but sea whips look like tiny fingers sticking up out of the sea floor.

ZEBRA SHARK: The young zebra shark has stripes, but those change into spots as it grows older. At night it hunts for mollusks, crustaceans, and small fish to eat.

The Crook and the Crown

Fit for a Princess

OH MY NEPTUNE! QUEEN Edwina sent her own royal carriage for us!" Pearl squealed.

Shelly Siren and her friends Pearl, Echo, and Kiki stood outside the Trident City People Museum as a large killer whale stopped beside them. The orca was pulling a sparkling shell carriage. Two tailmen wearing bright-blue coats with silver sashes lowered a glittering step from the carriage onto the ocean floor.

Another tailman, also wearing a blue coat, but with a gold sash, said in a loud voice, "Princess Shelly, it would be my honor to escort you and your servants to Neptune's Castle."

"Hey, we're not her servants!" Pearl snapped.

"It's all right, Pearl," Kiki said. "Let's just bubble down and enjoy the ride."

Pearl stuck her nose up in the water and frowned at the tailman but didn't complain anymore.

Shelly hugged her grandfather good-bye before floating up the carriage's diamond-covered stairs. The inside was just as beautiful as the outside. Blue gems lined the ceiling and the seats. Shelly could see her reflection shining in the walls.

"Ooh," Pearl said, running her hand over the jeweled seats. "I've heard of this. It's aquamarine and very rare in the ocean." She turned to Shelly. "This is a carriage fit for a princess! Good thing you *are* one!"

Shelly smiled, but inside she sure didn't feel like a princess! Still, her great-aunt was Queen Edwina of the Western Oceans, and that made her royalty.

As the carriage sped away, Shelly waved

to Grandfather Siren until she couldn't see him anymore. Then she sat back with a sigh. This was it! She was actually going to visit Neptune's Castle—the palace named for the very first king of the sea. When the queen had suggested that Shelly bring her friends to the castle during a school vacation, it had seemed exciting. Now it just felt scary.

Echo pushed back her dark, curly hair and turned to Shelly. "You're so quiet! Are you feeling all right?"

Shelly shrugged her blue tail. "I'm just nervous about visiting the castle. I'll be meeting all my cousins for the first time."

Even though her mother had been a princess, Shelly had only recently found out she was royal. Her parents had died when she was just a small fry, so Shelly had been raised by her grandfather in a tiny apartment in Trident City. She had never met her royal family, except for Queen Edwina.

"It's natural to be a little afraid," Kiki said. "But we'll be with you the whole time."

Shelly smiled. She knew her friends would do anything to make the visit a success.

Pearl shook her head, and her long blond hair swirled around her. "There's nothing to be worried about. We're going to a castle! There will be dinners and parties and everyone will want to meet us. They're going to love me—and you, too."

Shelly nodded and tried to act happy. But inside, her stomach felt like it was full of butterflyfish. After all, she'd much rather play on a Shell Wars team than wear a frilly party dress. And she wasn't sure if she could do the things a princess was supposed to do. What if she wasn't royal enough for her relatives?

Shelly's thoughts were interrupted by a squeal from Pearl.

"Sweet seaweed!" she gasped. "We're being invaded!"

Screech, Click, Squeal!

THE MERGIRLS LOOKED OUT the carriage window. They were surrounded by huge black-and-white killer whales!

"There are at least fifteen of them," Echo said, her dark eyes wide.

"They're going to kill us!" Pearl screeched.

Kiki shook her head. "Killer whales have never attacked merfolk before."

"Maybe they plan to start with us," Pearl said nervously, pushing away from the window and closing her eyes.

"I think they're beautiful," Shelly said, opening the carriage window and leaning out to watch the enormous creatures. Their fins were taller than her grandfather!

"Did you know that killer whales actually aren't whales at all?" Kiki told them. "They're the biggest of the dolphins."

"Did you know that I don't care?" Pearl snapped, her eyes still closed. "They're scary no matter what they are called!"

Suddenly, loud squealing noises filled the air.

Pearl put her hands over her ears. "What is that horrible racket?"

"The orcas are talking to each other," Shelly explained before making the same whistling noise. "They came to say hello!"

Kiki, Echo, and Pearl stared at Shelly in surprise.

"You know how to speak killer whale?" Kiki asked.

When Shelly nodded, Kiki said, "No wavy way! You have to teach me."

"Sure," Shelly said. She made a screech, followed by a click. "This means hello, nice to meet you." Kiki tried to do the same. Even Echo gave it a try, but Pearl frowned and sat with her ears covered, humming the newest song by the popular merboy band the Rays.

A chorus of sounds answered Shelly. She waved at the crowd of orcas near the carriage.

The killer whale pulling their carriage let out an especially loud whistle, and Shelly gulped. "We're almost there," she told her merfriends. "Our orca said to look to the right."

The mergirls leaned over to gaze out the window, and Shelly let out a cry.

"Oh my Neptune!"

"What's wrong?" Echo asked, peering over Shelly's shoulder. "It's beautiful!"

"It's enormous," Kiki said with a gulp.

Shelly nodded. "I knew it would be big, but this is grander than I ever dreamed."

All four mergirls stared out the windows as their carriage glided past large stone posts with fire spouting from them. Rows of spectacular seaweed formed paths that were dotted with statues, bubbling fountains, and coral displays. The gardens alone were overwhelming, but they led to a glistening castle that took Shelly's breath away.

Pearl gasped. "This is a mermillion times better than the drawings I've seen in *MerStyle* magazine. Check out that tower!"

Shelly looked up and down and all around. The palace had so many round buildings and domed roofs it was hard to take them all in. This was Neptune's famous castle! She couldn't believe she was in the place where the first king of the sea had lived many mercenturies ago.

"The windows really *are* made of blue sapphires—just like Mrs. Karp told us when we studied jewels," Kiki said.

A long line of merpeople stood in front of the large bronze castle door.

"Do you think those are my relatives?" Shelly whispered as their carriage slowed, then came to a stop.

Pearl shook her head. "No, those are probably the queen's merservants welcoming you." It was then that Shelly noticed the merpeople were wearing royal uniforms, some with aprons.

"But there are hundreds of them!" Echo told Pearl.

"Well, it is a big castle," Kiki said with a giggle.

Shelly looked at Kiki, and they both laughed. Echo chuckled too, but Pearl snapped her fingers. "This is no time for silliness. Inside the palace will be another line of people for you to meet—your royal family! Don't forget to curtsy to them."

Shelly stopped laughing. This was it! She was about to meet her many cousins. Her mind swirled with thoughts. What if they didn't like her? What if she wasn't royal enough? Did they know she had grown up in a tiny apartment instead of a gigantic castle? Suddenly Shelly wished more than anything that she had stayed home with her grandfather.

Debbie Dadey

is the author and coauthor of more than one hundred and sixty children's books, including the series The Adventures of the Bailey School Kids. A former teacher and librarian, Debbie and her family split their time between Bucks County, Pennsylvania, and Sevierville, Tennessee. She hopes you'll visit www.debbiedadey.com for lots of mermaid fun.

Candy Fairies

Chocolate Dreams

Rainbow Swirl

Caramel Moon

Cool Mint

Magic Hearts

Gooey Goblins

The Sugar Ball

A Valentine's Surprise

Bubble Gum Rescue

Double Dip

Jelly Bean Jumble

The Chocolate Rose

A Royal Wedding

Marshmallow Mystery

Frozen Treats

The Sugar Cup

Sweet Secrets

Taffy Trouble

Visit candyfairies.com for games, recipes, and more!

EBOOK EDITIONS ALSO AVAILABLE

FROM ALADDIN • KIDS.SIMONANDSCHUSTER.COM